TWO PINTS

RODDY DOYLE

Two Pints

JONATHAN CAPE
LONDON

Published by Jonathan Cape 2012

2 4 6 8 10 9 7 5 3

First published in Great Britain in 2012 by
Jonathan Cape

Random House, 20 Vauxhall Bridge Road,
London SW1V 2SA

www.vintage-books.co.uk

Addresses for companies within The Random House Group Limited
can be found at: www.randomhouse.co.uk/offices.htm

The Random House Group Limited Reg. No. 954009

A CIP catalogue record for this book
is available from the British Library

ISBN 9780224097819

The Random House Group Limited supports the Forest Stewardship
Council (FSC®), the leading international forest-certification organisation.
Our books carrying the FSC label are printed on FSC® certified paper.
FSC is the only forest-certification scheme endorsed by the leading
environmental organisations, including Greenpeace.
Our paper procurement policy can be found at
www.randomhouse.co.uk/environment

Typeset in Plantin by Palimpsest Book Production Limited,
Falkirk, Stirlingshire

Printed and bound in Great Britain by the MPG Books Group

For my brother, Shane

24-5-11

— Tha' was a great few days.

— Brilliant.

— She's a great oul' one. For her age, like.

— Fuckin' amazin'. Great energy.

— An' B'rack. He must've kissed every fuckin' baby in Offaly.

— An' did yeh see the way he skulled tha' pint?

— No doubtin' his fuckin' roots, an' anyway.

— An' the speech.

— Brilliant.

— 'Yes, we can' – whatever it is in Irish. He made the effort.

— What is it again?

— Haven't a clue. But it's funny, isn't it? Such a simple thing – a few speeches and smilin' faces. A bit of hope. An' it feels like we're over the worst, we've turned a corner.

— Exactly. It's great.

— We're still fucked but, aren't we?

— Bollixed.

— You know your man Gaddafi?

   — From the chipper?

   — No. The Libyan nut.

   — What about him?

   — You know the way they're lookin' for a country to take him?

   — I'm not in the mood for fuckin' politics.

   — He should come here.

   — Wha'?!

   — A state visit, like. The hat-trick. It'd be great. The few words of Irish, green jacket at the airport, kiss a few babies.

   — He'd strangle the fuckin' babies.

   — Not if he's looked after properly. It'd keep the buzz goin'. And the Shinners wouldn't object this time. He could bring the Semtex himself – save on the post.

   — Good point. Where's Libya, annyway?

   — I don't know – the desert.

   — Which one?

   — Wha'?

   — Which desert?

   — The fuckin' sandy one. Ask fuckin' Peter O'Toole.

6-6-11

— D'yeh know who'd make a fuckin' great president?

— Who?

— Your one who does the weather.

— Which one?

— The glamorous one – looks like she used to hang around with the Human League.

— She's lovely. Yeh'd give *her* one.

— I would, yeah. If I worked in the meteorological service. No, but she'd be great for the state visits an' tha'. She'd be able to point to the clouds an' say, 'That's a cold front comin' in from the south-west, Your Majesty. But it'll have fucked off by this afternoon.' Impress them, yeh know – a scientist in the Áras. An' she's a woman as well. They're always better at visitin' the homeless an' lookin' like they give a shite. An' she's a gay icon.

— What's a gay fuckin' icon?

— Somethin' all the gays like.

— Wha'? Like chicken curry?

— No – I don't know. I think it's more people – singers – women. Madonna an' tha'.

— Can she sing as well?

— Who?

— The weather one.

— More than likely.

— She could sing 'It's Rainin' Men' at the whatsit – the fuckin' inauguration.

— Good idea. An' at the airport, when the IMF fuckers are gettin' off the plane.

— Did you hear your man, the Senator, on the radio there?

— I fuckin' hate the radio. Which one?

— The one that's running for President. He was goin' on abou' Plato.

— The footballer?

— The ancient Greek – there's no footballer called Plato.

— I bet there is.

— Fuck up an' listen.

— In Brazil, somewhere.

— Shut up. He was sayin' abou' Plato. Young fellas came to him. Offerin' themselves, like. In return for sharing the wisdom of his fuckin' years. It was common enough – in ancient Greece.

— Wha' kind o' wisdom?

— I don't know – Remember to put the bins ou' the night before collection day. The bits of cop-on yeh pick up. In exchange for your moment of pleasure.

— Your moment of pleasure could go on all day, if you were talkin' abou' puttin' the fuckin' bins ou' while you were havin' it.

— Tha' was what I was thinkin'.

— The whole country would grind to a fuckin' standstill.

— I was thinkin' that as well.

— No wonder Greece is in fuckin' bits.

— I'm with yeh.

— Could they not have, like, just gone for a pint?

17-6-11

— See your man in America who twittered his dick.

— Wha'?

— The politician. Congressman or somethin'.

— Ah, not fuckin' politics again.

— No, listen. He sent his langer to some woman – by Twitter, yeh know?

— Cheaper than post, I suppose.

— A photograph, like.

— Wha' was he fuckin' up to?

— I'm not sure. I couldn't really figure it ou'.

— Well, I couldn't see any of our gang pullin' a stunt like tha', could you?

— They wouldn't have broadband, where most of them come from. The bog an' tha'.

— That's true.

— But I'll tell yeh one thing. They would, if they thought it would get them a few votes.

— That's true as well. Vote for me an' I'll come round to your house.

— Was it in the paper, was it?

— It was, yeah.

— Bet it didn't say langer or dick.

— No. Genitalia.

— It does nothin' for me, tha' word.

— I know what yeh mean. Are you on Twitter, yourself?

— Fuck off.

— We're after gettin' the Sky in.

   — Anny good?

   — Brilliant. The HD, yeh know. You can see fuckin' everythin'. On the news, like.

   — Ah fuck off now. Yeh don't need HD to watch the fuckin' news.

   — Will yeh just listen. Open your fuckin' head – for once.

   — Go on.

   — The riots.

   — They're back.

   — Big time. The Syrians. The Greeks.

   — Fuckin' wasters.

   — An' our own gang – above.

   — An' the riots are better on HD, are they?

   — It's not tha'. Some o' those black an' white riots – from the 60s. They're still brilliant. But it's the extra stuff.

   — Wha' extra stuff?

   — Well, like. I was watchin' the one in Belfast there. The first one. With the sound down. Mute, like. And I could still tell which side they were on. The young fellas throwin' the stones an' tha'. I knew they were fuckin' loyalists. Immediately.

   — How?

   — The tattoos. I could see every fuckin' one. Clear as if they were on me own arm here. UDA, No Surrender, The Pope's a Cunt – an' what have you.

   — Sounds good. Does it make the fuckin' economy look better as well?

   — Fuck off.

— How's the HD workin' out for yeh?

— Jesus, man, I'll tell yeh. It's fuckin' exhaustin'.

— How come?

— It's too real. Yeh can't relax. Every fuckin' spot an' ear hair. Your man, Richard Keys – they didn't sack him just cos he's a cunt. Tha' was just the excuse.

— He is a cunt, but.

— Ah yeah – no argument. But they got rid of him – the real reason – because he has hairy hands. A fuckin' werewolf interviewin' Beckham or wha'ever. They couldn't have it. That's why they're all gettin' Brazilians.

— On Sky Sports?!

— The gee hair, m'n – what's the official name for it? Pubic. It's Vietnam on HD.

— What fuckin' channels have yeh got?

— Yeh'd expect fuckin' Rambo to jump ou' – with his bandanna. Men as well – they're all gettin' it done. So I'm told an'anyway.

— Wha'?

— Gettin' the hair off. Arse hair as well. Drug dealers an' tha'.

— Wha?!

— In case they're caught on *Prime Time Investigates*. With the drugs hidden up there, like.

— They want to be lookin' their best.

— Exactly.

— It's not somethin' yeh'd want to do for a livin' but, is it?

— God, no – Jesus. If it can't go in the glove compartment, it isn't goin' annywhere.

— Would you be bothered hackin'?

— Hackin'?

— Yeah. Could yeh be bothered readin' your man, the black prostitute fella – what's his name? Hugh Grant. Would yeh really want to read his fuckin' texts?

— No.

— Me neither. Borin'.

— Unless it was somethin' unusual.

— Like wha'?

— Well, say he was stickin' it into Colette from the Mint or your woman with the hair from Paddy Power's. That'd be worth knowin' abou'.

— I'm with yeh.

— Other than tha' but—

— I've been hackin' me missis.

— There's plenty of her to hack.

— Fuck off now.

— Jesus, but. D'yeh have the technology an' tha' – to do it?

— I do, yeah.

— How d'yeh manage it?

— I read her texts when she goes to the jacks.

— Anny good ones?

— Not at all. The usual shite. Loads of fuckin' LOLs – an' the other one. PMSL. Don't know what it means.

— P is for period.

— An' M – that'll be the other one. Men's—

— Men's wha'?

— Menstruation.

— Makes sense. What about the S an' the L?

— Fuck knows.

— One thing.

— Wha'?

— How come yeh didn't slag my missis after I slagged yours?

— Are yeh ready for another pint?

— After yeh answer my fuckin' question.

13-7-11

— Harper Seven.

— I'm not listenin'.

— It's wha' Beckham an' Posh are after callin' their latest.

— I know.

— But, like – who gives a shite?

— Fuckin' everyone. In our house annyway.

— It's not a bad oul' name, really.

— It's the Seven bit's the problem.

— I know. But they prob'ly have their reasons. Somethin' sentimental.

— Like the amount o' times he had to ride her.

— I'll tell yeh. You're never fuckin' predictable.

— Fuck off. My brother's young one's little fella. John. Know wha' his full name is?

— Go on.

— John Player Blue.

— Fuck off.

— Swear to God. It's like I said. Sentimental reasons. They met outside the boozer a few weeks after the smokin' ban kicked in. And John arrived soon after.

— That's kind o' nice.

— There now.

— They still together?

— No. Actually – he died. The husband.

— That's rough.

— Cancer. She was pregnant as well. A girl. Know wha' she called her?

— Wha'?

— Cancer.

— Fuck off now. I'm not listenin' to yeh.

— A tribute to his memory.

— Fuck off.
— D'yeh want to know the surname?
— No.
— Ward.
— Cancer Ward?
— A lovely kid. A breath of fresh air.
— Fuck off.

— How come the most borin' stuff is the most important?

— Wha' d'yeh mean?

— Well, look it. What's the best thing yeh saw on the news this week?

— Murdoch's missis slappin' the comedian.

— Me too. It was fuckin' brilliant. An' I bet you were sittin' there watchin', and wishin' your missis was Chinese. Amn't I righ'?

— Kind o'.

— Fuckin' sure I am. She threw her whole body into tha' slap. But – this is my point. It doesn't matter a fuck. It was only a laugh. But, now, all the EU leaders meetin' in Brussels tomorrow—

— Ah, fuck off. I'm not interested in those cunts.

— Exactly my point. The thought of it – it makes me want to lie down an' fuckin' die. But it's vital.

— Why?

— I don't fuckin' know. I just know it is. But the thought of tryin' to understand it – defaultin', an' Greece, an' all tha' shite.

— If they brought their wives an' husbands—

— That's it. Human interest. Sittin' behind them, like Murdoch's. An' Merkel says somethin' snotty abou' Ireland—

— Kenny's wife slaps her across the fuckin' head.

— Yeh'd watch.

— I might.

— Yeh fuckin' would.

— Okay.

25-7-11

— Did yeh like Amy?

   — I did, yeah.

   — A bit skinny.

   — Great fuckin' voice.

   — True.

   — Sad.

   — Desperate. The same age as my oldest.

   — A real singer. None o' the *X Factor* shite.

   — No.

   — Horrible week.

   — Fuckin' awful.

   — Norway.

   — Frightenin'.

   — Who'd shoot kids?

   — I haven't a clue.

   — Horrible.

   — Fuckin' horrible.

   — An' Somalia.

   — Stop.

   — Where is Somalia, exactly?

   — I don't even know where Norway is, exactly.

— Well, at least we have the cunts in the Vatican to give us a laugh.

   — I'm not laughin'.

   — The fuckin' heads on them.

— Thank Christ the football's back in a couple o' weeks.

— What're yeh sayin'? Tha' none o' this would've happened if there'd been football on the telly?

   — Fuck off. It's not funny.

   — You're righ'. Sorry.

   — Okay.

— No massacres this week.

— Stop tha'.

— Were you across at Amy's funeral?

— I'll leave, I'm fuckin' tellin' yeh.

— Okay. Fair enough. Wha' abou' the ban on smokin' in cars? Can I mention tha'?

— It should be up to the kids.

— Wha'?

— The ban. It's when there are children in the vehicle, righ'?

— Righ'.

— So, the children should vote on it. In the back o' the car, like.

— They'd bribe the poor fucker tha' wants a smoke.

— Exactly. It'd teach them to be adults. Cash only. In little brown child-sized envelopes.

— You're not jokin'.

— No way am I. It's the problem with this fuckin' country. We're tryin' not to be corrupt. But we should be teachin' our kids to be even more corrupt. Like every other country in the world. Not just Greece an' the mad places – fuckin' everywhere. They're laughin' at us.

— I don't know. Yeh might have a point.

— I do have a fuckin' point.

— What if there's only one kid in the car?

— Then the dopey prick drivin' it should have no problem countin' the votes.

15-8-11

— How did Wexford go for yeh?

— I'll tell yeh. We were sittin' in the mobile, myself and herself. Watchin' the news. Cos it was fuckin' bucketin' outside. There's the riots in London. Then there's this stuff abou' how the euro is basically fucked. So she says, Fuck it, let's blow it. So, that's wha' we do. We get the Tesco bus into Gorey and we fuckin' spend it.

— Your jeans are new.

— Fuck off a minute. We're in this pub, Browne's, and we go out for a smoke. She takes ou' her BlackBerry an' she taps in some fuckin' thing. An' she puts up the hood of her pink hoodie. An' then – basically – she's gone. Like a fuckin' greyhound. Across to this shoe shop. Gaffney's. She takes a run at it an' kicks the fuckin' window.

— Did she break it?

— She missed it. But she has another go. An' then there are other women – middle-aged, like. An' they're all kickin' the window. They're only up from the fuckin' Garda station. An' sure enough, here's a Guard, an' they leg it. I haven't seen her since. Where were you, yourself?

— Magaluf.

— Where's tha'?

— I'm not sure – we went in a plane.

22-8-11

— I was ou' at the airport there.

— Doin' wha'?

— Lookin' at the boats – wha' d'yeh think I was fuckin' doin'?

— I don't know. Goin' somewhere, comin' back. Fuckin' lay off.

— We were ou' meeting her sister.

— Comin' back from somewhere.

— Yeah.

— Where?

— Can't remember – doesn't matter. We're at the arrivals place, yeh know, and I'm bored out of me fuckin' tree, cos her flight's late. So I start doin' imaginary passport control as all the people are comin' in off the planes – in me head, like. You can stay, you can stay, you can fuck off, you can stay. An' anyway, that's when I see him.

— Who?

— Gaddafi.

— From the chipper?

— No, the other one. From Libya.

— In Dublin Airport?

— Terminal 2.

— Fuck off.

— Swear to God. That's where he's hidin'.

— Fuckin' hell. An' he'd just arrived, had he?

— No, this is the genius bit. He was moppin' the floor.

— Gaddafi was?

— Fuckin' brilliant, isn't it?

— Colonel Gaddafi?

— They'll never find him there.

— You're sure it was him?

— Course I am. I winked at him.
— Wha' did he do?
— He winked back.

— That's a fuckin' jumper.

    — Birthday present.

    — Purple's your colour.

    — Fuck off.

    — I'm serious. Man o' your age. It's brave.

    — Fuck off.

    — D'yeh get annythin' else?

    — This.

    — Wha'?

    — This – hang on. I've to get it – it's around me neck.

    — What's tha'?

    — Kind of a dog tag.

    — What's it say there? I am neutered and chipped. It *is* a fuckin' dog tag.

    — Yeah.

    — Who fuckin' gave yeh tha'?

    — She did.

    — Why, but?

    — She got it off the dog. She died, like.

    — Your missis?

    — No, the fuckin' dog. A few months ago there. D'yeh remember?

    — I do now, yeah. What was it again?

    — Mongrel – bits of fuckin' everythin'.

    — No, wha' killed it, I meant.

    — Ah, just fuckin' fat – yeh know yourself. Great oul' dog, but. An' anyway, she held on to the collar.

    — That's nice. Considerate.

    — I thought so. An' that's not all. The chain.

    — What about it?

    — Gold.

    — No.

— Yeah. Her idea. Somethin' she heard on the radio. It'll hold its value long after the euro goes down the fuckin' jacks.

— So, it's not just romantic.

— It's me fuckin' pension. An' it's goin' back under me new purple jumper.

— I need this pint.

— I know.

— No. I really need it.

— Yeh look a bit flaked alrigh'. Wha' were yeh up to?

— Writin' my response to the Vatican.

— Wha'?!

— Well, like, I responded to the Vatican's response yesterday to Enda fuckin' Kenny's response to the child abuse inquiry in – it'll come back to me in a minute – Cloyne.

— Say tha' again. No – don't. But. Am I righ'? You wrote to the fuckin' Vatican.

— I did, yeah.

— To the fuckin' Pope.

— Yeah.

— Fuckin' hell – fair play. Wha' did yeh say?

— Fuck off.

— I was only askin'.

— No. That's wha' I said. Tha' was my response. And I think I spoke on behalf of the vast majority of the Irish people. The Dubs an'anyway.

— You told the Pope to fuck off?

— I did, yeah.

— How?

— The usual way.

— Yeh shouted? He wouldn't have heard yeh from here.

— No, email.

— You emailed the Pope?

— I did, yeah.

— Fuckin' hell. Did he answer?

— Not yet. Come here, but. Yeh know the way you're

angry sometimes but yeh cop on an' calm down. But other times you're angry an' yeh know you're righ' to be.

— Yeah.

— Yeah, well, this was one o' those times.

8-9-11

— Did the Pope get back to yeh yet?

— He did, yeah – this mornin'.

— Did he? Jesus. Wha' did he say?

— Well – like, it was in Latin.

— D'you know any Latin?

— We wouldn't speak it much at home, no. But listen. I found this English–Latin dictionary yoke. Google, like. An' there's a box for the Latin. So, I typed in his – the fuckin' Pope's email – it's only short. An' the English came up.

— Wha' did it say?

— Tell your sister I was asking for her.

— Fuckin' hell. The Pope wrote tha'?

— In fuckin' Latin.

— So, wha' did yeh do?

— I told me sister – I phoned her. I knew which one he meant.

— And wha' did she say?

— Tell him he was a terrible ride an' he can fuck off back to Poland.

— Tha' was the last one.

— Tha' was the one she meant, I think. So, annyway, I translated it into Latin an' sent it to the fuckin' Vatican. An' I said I expected a reasoned response by the end o' the week.

— He'll deny he's Polish.

— I cheated there. I changed it to German.

— He can't deny he's German.

— No, but he mightn't admit it, either. They're slippy fuckers.

— Have yeh recovered yet?

— Ah fuck, man. What a day. I'm still a bit – I don't fuckin' know – overwhelmed.

— Know wha' yeh mean. I had to lie down on the bed for a bit.

— I cried.

— Me too.

— Fuckin' hell.

— I never thought I'd see it happen again.

— No – same here. It's been so long – I'd given up hopin'.

— But the way he took tha' ball.

— Incredible.

— Fuckin' incredible. Here, look it. Give us a hug.

— Hang on, hang on. You're not upstairs in the fuckin' lounge.

— Sorry.

— No, you're grand. Have a suck o' your pint.

— Yeah – thanks.

— You're grand.

— Somethin' to tell the grandkids, wha'.

— Exactly, yeah.

— We saw it.

— That's it. The day Fernando Torres scored a fuckin' goal.

Man Utd 3–1 Chelsea

— Who'll yeh be votin' for?

    — Fuck tha' – not interested.

    — Come on. Be a citizen. There's the Senator.

    — Which one's he?

    — The James Joyce wanker.

    — Got yeh. He did somethin', didn't he?

    — He wrote a letter defendin' an Israeli paedophile.

    — Could he not've defended one of our own paedophiles?

    — His patriotic duty. I never saw it tha' way before.

    — Who else is runnin'?

    — Dana.

    — Ah, for fuck sake. Louis Walsh in a fuckin' dress. Who else?

    — McGuinness.

    — Has he given up managin' U2?

    — Different McGuinness.

    — The Provo?

    — He says he left them in 1974.

    — He's lying through his arse, so. No change there. Who else?

    — Your man from *Dragons' Den*.

    — Tha' cunt?

    — He says he won't be havin' anny posters.

    — Not surprised, the fuckin' head on him. Who else?

    — Gay Mitchell.

    — For fuck—. Who else?

    — Michael D. Higgins.

    — Which one's he?

    — Squeaky voice, poetry, Nicaragua.

    — Is he still alive?

    — At the moment, yeah – far as I know.

— Who else?

— Mary Davis.

— Who?

— Special Olympics.

— Did she win a medal?

— She ran the thing – organised it. Yeh feel guilty now, don't yeh?

— No.

— Yeh feel horrible.

— I don't – fuck off.

— Yeh do – go on.

— Okay, I do – fuck off.

— Have yeh made your mind up yet?

— A pint – same as always. I haven't had to make me mind up since—

— I meant the election.

— Ah, shove it.

— Well, it's either tha' or the Greek default.

— Alrigh' – fuck it. Who's goin' to win?

— Hard to say. They're all shite.

— I seen Mary Davis's *Sex an' the City* posters.

— There yeh go. An' Mitchell. He said you can see the house he grew up in – in Inchicore, like – from the window of the Áras. An' he's goin' to look out at it every mornin'.

— An' shout, Fuck you, Inchicore.

— He could get the Queen to do it with him the next time she's over.

— A bondin' exercise.

— Exactly. She probably never gets the chance to say Fuck at home.

— Talkin' abou' fuck an' the Queen. What's McGuinness up to?

— Says he'll only pay himself the average industrial wage.

— The fuckin' eejit.

— I'm with yeh. He says he'll employ six young people with the money left over.

— Cuttin' the grass an' washin' diesel. What about the Senator?

— Ah Jaysis. It looks like Greece is goin' to miss its deficit target an' has fuck-all chance of avertin' bankruptcy.

— Wha' d'yeh think of the poll?

    — He's alrigh'. He pulls a reasonable pint.

    — I meant, the election poll.

    — Ah, fuck the—. Go on.

    — Michael D.'s leadin'.

    — Followed by Mitchell.

    — No. The *Dragons' Den* fella.

    — Fuckin' hell. How did tha' happen?

    — Well, he's scutterin' on abou' community an' disability an' tha'. But, really, he's an ol' Fianna Fáil hack. Up to his entrepreneurial bollix in it. Annyway, my theory.

    — Go on.

    — People still love Fianna Fáil.

    — But they'd hammer them if they had a candidate.

    — Exactly. But they can vote for this prick without havin' to admit it.

    — Brilliant.

    — But I think Michael D. will get there.

    — How come?

    — He was goin' on abou' the President not bein' a handmaiden to the government.

    — What's a handmaiden?

    — I'm not sure. But if I was lookin' for one in the Golden Pages, I wouldn't be stoppin' at the Michaels. Annyway, he suddenly stops, an' says he broke his kneecap when he fell durin' a fact-findin' mission in Colombia. Wha' does tha' tell yeh?

    — He was ou' of his head.

    — Exactly. Fact-findin' mission me hole. He's lettin' us know – he's one o' the lads.

    — Well, that's me decided.

    — Me too.

— Tha' must've been some party.

— Wha' party?

— The one in Tallaght. Five stabbin's.

— Is tha' your idea of a good party?

— Not necessarily, no. An' I didn't say it was 'good', so fuck off.

— Well, I'm sorry. And?

— An' wha'?

— Wha's your fuckin' point?

— Well, for a start. I thought you'd be happy tha' I'm not talkin' about the fuckin' election.

— Oh, I am.

— Grand. So, annyway. It said on the news tha' they were taken – the ones tha' got stabbed, like – to different hospitals, to make sure there wouldn't be a continuation of the hostilities.

— Well, tha' makes sense.

— Exactly. That's what I thought. The thinkin' tha' went into it. The infrastructional plannin'.

— The wha'?

— When they were buildin' Tallaght hospital, they must've thought, we'd better leave James' Street open as well, just in case.

— In case there's a scrap?

— You're with me. An', well – I think that's worth celebratin'. Cos we don't hear enough good news these days – fuckin' success stories.

— So. You're sayin' we should celebrate five stabbin's in Tallaght?

— It's only a fuckin' suggestion.

— D'yeh ever read poetry?

— Wha'?!

— D'you ever—

— I heard yeh. I just can't fuckin' believe I heard yeh.

— Well, look it—

— G'wan upstairs to the lounge if yeh want to talk abou' poetry.

— Just let me—

— Unless yeh can talk abou' the football in rhyme. 'There was a young player called Blunt'.

— There's no player called Blunt – far as I know.

— You're missin' me point.

— I'm not. I heard yeh. Yeh didn't hear me.

— I did.

— You feel threatened by it.

— No, I don't.

— Yeh do. Yeh even moved your stool there.

— I didn't.

— Yeh fuckin' did. To get away from anny mention of poetry. It's mad.

— Well, it's a load o' shite.

— I agree with yeh. That's wha' I'm tryin' to say.

— Yeh've lost me now.

— So listen. My young's one's youngest lad, Damien.

— The kid with the cheeks.

— That's him. He's good in school – the great white hope. Annyway, he has to read a fuckin' poem an' write a bit about it. The homework, like.

— Okay.

— So, he's in our place, cos his ma's visitin' the da. An' he asks me to, yeh know, look at the poem. So I get the oven gloves on an' I give it a dekko. 'The Road Not

Taken' – some bollix called Robert Frost. Have yeh read it, yourself?

— I won't even say no.

— Two roads diverged in a yellow wood. Stay where yeh are; I'm just givin' yeh a flavour o' the thing.

— And – wha'?

— Well, this cunt – Robert Frost, like – he's makin' his mind up abou' which road to take an' he knows he'll regret not takin' one o' them. An' that's basically it.

— He doesn't need a fuckin' poem for tha'. That's life. It's common fuckin' sense.

— Exactly. I go for the cod, I regret the burger.

— I married the woman but I wish I could be married to her sister.

— Is tha' true?

— Not really – no.

— Annyway. Yeh sure?

— Go on.

— So annyway, the poor little bollix – Damien, like – the grandson. He has to answer questions about it. An' the last one – it's really stupid now. What road do you think you should never take? An', like, I tell him, The road to Limerick.

— Did he write tha'?

— He fuckin' did. An' guess where the fuckin' teacher comes from? An' guess who's been called up to the fuckin' school, to explain himself to the fuckin' headmaster?

— Brilliant.

— Tomorrow mornin'.

— Serves yeh righ' for readin' poetry.

— I agree. A hundred fuckin' per cent. Two roads diverged in a yellow wood me hole.

— Wha' d'yeh think o' Dana's sister sayin' that her –

— No! No – please—

— Okay.

— Thanks.

— Can I just say one thing abou' Miriam O'Callaghan's outrageous bullyin' of poor Martin McGuinness in the *Prime Time* debate? An' then we'll move on.

— Okay. One thing.

— Only one – thanks. She can bully me anny time she fuckin' wants.

— That it?

— That's it.

— The first sensible thing yeh've said in weeks.

— Months.

— Ever.

22-10-11

— So Gaddafi's gone.

— From the chipper?

— Ah, listen – look it. You're goin' to have to broaden your fuckin' horizons.

— Oh, the other one.

— Yeah, the other one.

— Yeah, I seen tha'. The man with the golden gun.

— Didn't do him much fuckin' good, did it? See they found him in a drainage pipe?

— Yeah.

— I'll tell yeh. The last couple o' months must've been rough. Cos he wouldn't've fitted into tha' pipe a few months back.

— We'll kind o' miss him.

— We will in our holes. An' d'yeh see ETA's declared a ceasefire?

— Thank fuck. That's great news.

— Oh, you're interested in tha' one, are yeh?

— Fuckin' sure – the noise she was makin'.

— Hang on – wha'?

— A woman of her age, buyin' a fuckin' drum kit with her redundancy – her fuckin' lump sum. Thinks she's Keith fuckin' Moon at three in the fuckin' mornin'.

— Hang on—

— It's a disgrace.

— Hang on. Not Eithne.

— Oh.

— ETA.

— The Spanish cunts who aren't Spanish.

— Exactly.

— Shite.

1-11-11

— Wha' does 'thinkin' outside the box' mean?

— You were watchin' *The Apprentice* last night, weren't yeh?

— I was, yeah.

— Me too.

— Wouldn't've thought it was your cup o' tea.

— It isn't. But we had to give the dog half a Valium, cos of all the fuckin' bangers and fireworks. An' he conked ou' on top o' me. So I was stuck – couldn't reach the remote.

— Yeh saw it, so.

— Load o' shite.

— I'm with yeh. But they're all runnin' around – the contestants, like – an' they're all, I'm thinkin' outside the box, Bill. What's it fuckin' mean?

— Comin' up with somethin' new. Thinkin' a bit different.

— That all?

— Think so.

— For fuck sake.

— Last time I thought outside the box I tried to get off with me mother-in-law.

— Fuck off.

— Before she died, mind.

— Ah, fuck off. I'll give yeh an example. My young one's lad. Damien. The grandson. He goes into the chipper, with his chipmunk.

— His—?

— Chipmunk. An' he tells Gaddafi he'll fuck it into the fryer unless Gaddafi pays him a tenner.

— I'm impressed. And?

— Gaddafi tells him to fuck off.

33

— And?
— D'yeh ever taste deep-fried chipmunk?
— That's thinkin' outside the snack box.
— It fuckin' is.

— So annyway, I was listenin' to the news there.

— Oh fuck.

— No, fuck off a minute. This is important. *Morning Ireland*, it was. The posh news.

— Go on.

— An' the headline – this was one o' the headlines. Italian parliament under pressure to take out Berlusconi. Take out was wha' he said, the news cunt. An' he didn't mean bringin' him ou' for a nosebag an' a few drinks in the lounge.

— He meant kill him.

— Assassinate him, yeah.

— Why would the Italian parliament be under pressure to assassinate Michael Jackson's doctor?

— Wha'?

— Berlusconi is Wacko's—

— You're gettin' your stories mixed up.

— Got yeh there, bud.

— Ah, fuck off. So, annyway. There's that. The *inappropriate* language. An' then there's the story itself.

— How d'yeh mean?

— Well, the bondholders aren't happy with Berlusconi, so he has to go. But then I'm thinkin', just who do these fuckin' cuntin' poxy bondholders think they fuckin' are? Berlusconi's a prick but he's an elected prick. Who elected the bondholders? Fuckin' no one.

— Were yeh a Frazier or an Ali man?

— Frazier. An' the Stones.

— I was Ali. An' the Beatles.

— Go upstairs to the lounge, where yeh fuckin' belong.

12-11-11

— Are yeh goin' to Poland?

— I'm only after gettin' back from the jacks. Give us a fuckin' chance.

— I meant the football, yeh gobshite.

— I know yeh did, yeh cunt.

— Well, are yeh?

— Don't think so. It's cold there, isn't it?

— Not in fuckin' June – I don't think.

— Summer there then, is it?

— I'd say so, yeah.

— I'll tell yeh wha' it is. The football's shite. The way we play.

— It's always been shite. We play ugly.

— We are fuckin' ugly.

— That's it – spot on. We're the ugliest cunts on the planet and we still sing. Especially when there's a recession.

— The Mexicans are way uglier than us.

— That's fuckin' debatable.

— No way is it. They're un-fuckin'-believable. And the Welsh.

— The fuckin' Welsh?

— Yeah. You know your man, the Snag? He's over there, beside the picture of the Dubs. Don't look – don't fuckin' look!

— Is he Welsh?

— No, but he was conceived in Holyhead when his ma an' da missed the ferry.

— Ah, fuck off. It's great but, isn't it? Qualifyin' for the football.

— It is, yeah.

— Gives the place a lift.
— It's not as good as the Queen's visit, but.
— Fuck, no. Tha' was the best.

Estonia 0–4 Republic of Ireland

— Will the euro last?

   — I've enough left for a couple o' pints, an'anyway.

   — I mean the currency. Is it fucked?

   — I don't care.

   — Ah, fuck tha'. Yeh have to have an opinion.

   — Why should I? Fuck it.

   — But—

   — We were able to enjoy the occasional pint before the euro. Yeah?

   — Yeah.

   — We'll still be able to do tha' if the euro goes. Life'll go on.

   — You're righ'.

   — Wha'?

   — You're probably righ'.

   — I am.

   — We'll still be able to buy Cornettos for the grandkids when they come over on Sundays.

   — No fuckin' way.

   — Ah now, would yeh begrudge—

   — It's Magnums in our house.

   — Yeh posh cunts.

   — It's Magnums or nothin'. I told her. If we can't afford Magnums for the grandkids, we might as well turn on the gas.

   — Yeh don't want to be too hasty. There mightn't be anny in the shop.

   — Yeh know what I mean.

   — I do, yeah.

   — Every Sunday. Magnums for everyone. Even the youngest. She's lactose-intolerant, God love her. Yeh should see the state of her by the time she's finished. Try

takin' it off it her, but – she'll bite your ankle through to
the bone.
    — She has respect for family tradition.
    — She fuckin' does.

29-11-11

— Did yeh get tha' flu yet?

— You've been its victim, yeah?

— Did yeh not notice I wasn't here?

— I thought yeh'd gone quiet alrigh'.

— Fuck off now. It was fuckin' desperate. I had a temperature of 123.

— Is tha' fuckin' possible?

— So she said, an'annyway. An' she gave the yoke a good shake before she put it under me arm.

— Yeh can't argue with science.

— That's another thing.

— Wha'?

— I'm in the bed, feelin' woegious. An' there's this smell. Un-fuckin'-believable. First of all, I think it's me. But it's comin' from downstairs. So I go down. I have to cling to the banister, the sweat's drippin' off me. An' young Damien's in the kitchen – the grandson, like. An' there's a mouse in the fuckin' toaster.

— Ah Jaysis.

— So I say it must have fallin' in – to comfort him, like. But he says, No, Granda, I thrun it in.

— Is this the same lad tha' threw the chipmunk into the deep-fat fryer?

— That's him.

— Do yeh detect a fuckin' pattern here?

— He's goin' to be a scientist – a biologist.

— D'yeh reckon?

— Fuckin' sure. We can all love animals, yeah?

— I suppose.

— Well, Damien takes it further. He's curious abou' them.

— Isn't it great tha' we can hate the Brits again?

— Brilliant, yeah. It's a load off me mind.

— Good oul' Cameron.

— The baby-faced prick. Wha' is it he's after vetoin', exactly?

— I haven't a fuckin' clue. It doesn't matter.

— Fuckin' gas, isn't it?

— Brilliant. All tha' matters is tha' the news will make sense from now on. The Brits will be to blame for everythin'.

— It's fuckin' great. After three years of not understandin' wha' was happenin'. Now but. The bondholders.

— Brits.

— Every fuckin' one o' them.

— The Brits are to blame for where we are now.

— Yep.

— And for blockin' all attempts to get us ou' of our fuckin' predicament.

— Bastards.

— I love them.

— All the Queen's hard work – up in smoke.

— Thank fuck. It was too complicated. But do we have to start hatin' her again as well?

— There's always a downside, unfortunately.

— The fuckin' wagon.

— Good man. You're adaptin' to the new reality.

— I fuckin' am.

— You're a good European.

— Come here, but. It's a pity Cameron isn't Thatcher, isn't it?

— Ah, Jaysis. I've died an' gone to heaven.

— My pint's not the best. How's yours?

— Only so-so.
— The fuckin' Brits.
— Cunts.

— See the Queen's goin' to mention Ireland in her Christmas speech.

    — Ah, great. I might mention her in mine.

    — It's a big deal.

    — Not really. I just say a few words to the family.

    — The Queen's one, I meant.

    — Fuck 'er – she has it easy.

    — She's goin' to say Ireland's great or somethin'.

    — She can hardly say we're a bunch o' cunts.

    — They'd sit up an' listen.

    — That's my point. They won't sit up when she says we're grand. It's borin'. I suppose yeh have all your presents bought, do yeh?

    — The ones I didn't rob.

    — Yeh girl.

    — Fuck off.

    — Wha' did yeh get young Damien? A wolf?

    — God, no. Nothin' like tha'.

    — Wha' then?

    — A hyena.

    — Where the fuck did yeh get a hyena?

    — Wicklow. There's a fella rears them – in a caravan, like.

    — Where is it now?

    — In the attic.

    — Does Damien know?

    — Not yet. But he stayed with us there a few weeks ago. An' he tells me tha' the hyena's reputation for bein' a scavenger isn't deserved. Tha' they kill 95 per cent of wha' they eat. Yeh should've heard him. Like fuckin' Attenborough.

    — An' it's in your attic?

— Yeah.

— Gift-wrapped?

— Not yet, no. That's her department.

— Are yeh all set for the Christmas?

— Fuck the Christmas.

— Ah now—

— There was no way he was the son of God.

— Who?

— Jesus.

— Which one?

— Wha'?

— Which Jesus, like? You man over there or the Israeli fella?

— The Israeli, o' course. Your man over there – that's only his nickname. His ma was called Mary an' the postman's name was Joe. His real name's Larry. Annyway, Christmas is a load o' bollix.

— Is your eldest comin' home this year?

— No.

— Too far?

— Yeah. So he says.

— Where is it he's gone again?

— Drogheda.

— That's only up—

— I'm messin'. Melbourne.

— New Zealand.

— Exactly. Nearly all his pals have gone. All over the place. An' there now. Jesus. Jesus over there, like. His lad – Danny. D'yeh know wha' he's up to?

— Wha'?

— He's a Somali pirate.

— Fuck off.

— True as God. He saw it on the news an' liked the sound of it. So off he went.

— Did he do a course or somethin'?

— Not before he left – far as I know. I don't think there's a piracy course here. Yet.

— He'll hardly be home for the Christmas.

— No, this is their busy time.

— So. The high points an' the low points of last year.

— No fuckin' way.

— Ah, go on.

— Listen, bud. I already have me low point for this fuckin' year.

— Christ – sorry. Wha' happened?

— Young Damien's hyena.

— Go on.

— I had to put him out of his misery this mornin'. The hyena, like. Not Damien.

— Was it sick?

— Not really.

— Wha' happened?

— Well, the hyena was Damien's Crimbo present, like. Yeh remember tha'?

— I do, yeah.

— So, all's grand – on the day itself. The fuckin' thing never stopped laughin'. It was fuckin' gas, actually. Burstin' its shite laughin'. Even durin' *Downton Abbey*. An' tha' takes some doin'. Laughin' through tha' shite. Annyway but, the trouble starts the day after. When Damien lets it ou' the back for a dump.

— Oh God.

— Rita next door. Her chickens, yeah?

— Gone.

— You betcha. An' Larry Hennessey's English bulldog.

— Fuckin' hell.

— I'm not finished.

— Go on.

— One o' Stella Caprani's twins.

— It didn't eat a fuckin' twin.

— Not all of it – in fairness. A fair bit, though. So annyway. Tha' was tha'.

— How did yeh do it?

— Shovel – the usual.

— Sad.

— Desperate.

— Poor Damien.

— Ah, he'll be grand. He has his eye on a gorilla.

16-1-12

— You're like me, I'd say, are yeh?

— I fuckin' hope not. How?

— Yeh hate havin' your dinner interrupted.

— Well, yeah. I'm with yeh there. Definitely.

— It drives me spare.

— Me too. The bell, the phone – they can fuck off till I'm done.

— Same here.

— Sometimes, like, she even expects me to talk to her. While I'm eatin', yeh know.

— It's fuckin' unbelievable. Annyway. You're just startin' the dinner when the cruiser hits the rocks. Do yeh finish it or leg it to the lifeboats?

— Depends. Wha' is it?

— Risotto.

— What's tha'?

— Rice.

— On its own?

— No. It's nice. Like Chinese, except it's Italian.

— I'll finish it, so. Anny idea what else was on the menu?

— No. It just said risotto in the paper.

— Grand. An' I wouldn't rush it either. We don't want heartburn.

— We'd eat first, then climb over the women an' children to get to the lifeboats. Like the lads – the crew, like.

— My fuckin' heroes.

— Especially the captain.

— Francesco Schettino.

— They should put him in charge o' the euro.

— He'd know when to quit.

— He fuckin' would.

24-1-12

— Wha' d'yeh think of cancer?

— I'm all for it.

— I'm serious.

— Well, like – what's there to think?

— Which one would yeh prefer? If yeh had to choose, like?

— Well, definitely not the balls.

— We're too old for tha' one.

— Really?

— Yeah.

— Fuckin' great. How d'yeh know, but?

— Me cousin. He had to have a medical an' they told him, an' he's the same age as us.

— That's great. What's left?

— Bowels.

— God, no.

— It's not usually fatal.

— Don't care. I'd prefer the lungs.

— That's one o' the worst.

— I don't give a shite. It has more style.

— Wha'?!

— Okay. Listen. Say you're chattin' to a bird. Your missis has died or somethin'. Whatever – and you're chattin' to this woman. You tell her you have lung cancer, you're home an' dry. She'll think you're Humphrey Bogart. But tell her you've bowel cancer?

— She's gone.

— Exactly.

— What about prostate?

— I'm not even sure what it is. What's it do?

— Don't know. Me cousin said it's the one we should be worried about. At our age, like.

— What's the test?
— Finger up the hole.
— Doctor's finger?
— Yeah, has to be a doctor. It's fifty quid extra for two fingers. The cousin said.

1-2-12

— Would you ever let yourself be digitally enhanced?

— Wha'?

— Would you ever—

— I heard yeh, but wha' the fuck are yeh talkin' abou'?

— You're chosen to be the face of L'Oréal.

— Me?

— Yeah. So—

— L'Oréal. That's the butter tha' spreads straight from the fridge.

— No—

— Wha' would they want my fuckin' face for?

— It's not – You know fuckin' well what it is.

— Go on. They've called to the house an' asked me to be their face. An' I've said, Yeah. Have I?

— Yeah.

— Grand. Go on.

— So they do the shoot – the filmin', like.

— 'Because you're worth it.' How was tha'?

— Very good.

— Did it give yeh the horn?

— Not really.

— Okay. I'll put the pint closer to me lips. Because you're well fuckin' worth it. Better?

— I felt a bit of a tingle tha' time, alrigh'. But annyway, they decide to digitally enhance yeh. Like they did with Rachel Weisz.

— Rachel – ?

— Stay with me. They decide to make yeh look younger.

— Wha'? Fifty-four, like?

— Forty.

— Fuckin' great.

— Is it not unethical, but?

— What age is Rachel?
— Forty-two.
— Does she go for younger men?
— She might.
— Well then. Unethical, me hole.

12-2-12

— Poor oul' Whitney, wha'.

— Sad.

— Desperate.

— She was a great young one.

— She was forty-eight.

— But she was always a young one. D'yeh know what I mean?

— An' forty-eight's young these days annyway.

— True. She's at home, fuckin' devastated.

— Whitney?

— Stop bein' thick. The wife. She felt a special – I don't know – a link, I suppose. Our youngest, Kevin, yeh know – he was conceived after we saw *The Bodyguard*.

— In the fuckin' cinema?

— No, we made it home. Well – the front garden.

— Nice one.

— We stopped at the boozer – here actually, upstairs. An' the chipper.

— Romantic.

— Fuck off. The chips were her idea.

— The ride was yours, but, was it?

— No, no. She took the initiative there as well. Thing was, she thought the fillum was the best thing she'd ever seen an' I thought it was a load o' shite.

— Bet you didn't tell her that.

— I forgot. So anyway, Kevin arrived the nine months later.

— Hang on. Kevin Costner.

— Exactly; yeah.

— An' if he'd been a girl, it would've been—

— Whitney; yeah.

— Ah God. I'm sorry for your troubles, bud.

— Thanks.

— D'yeh know the way they're thinkin' o' frackin' Leitrim?

— I can't believe I understood tha' question. But, yeah.

— An' you know what frackin' involves, do yeh?

— Kind o' – yeah.

— Well, young Damien reckons we'd find gas in our back if we fracked it.

— Does he?

— So he says. All the animals we've buried ou' there. The hyena an' tha'. Remember?

— I do, yeah.

— Well, he says there should be enough gas to supply our road. So, like – I left him to it.

— Hang on. Young Damien is frackin' your back garden?

— Yeah.

— What's he usin'.

— Her Magimix.

— Is she happy with tha'?

— She doesn't know. She's still over at Whitney's funeral.

— So she went?

— She did, yeah. Cleaned ou' the fuckin' credit union. But I'm worried. About the frackin', like.

— Why?

— Well, it's – like – controversial, isn' it? An' dangerous. I don't want to, yeh know, impede young Damien's natural curiosity, but we could've gas comin' out the fuckin' taps. There was a fella, a geologist like, on *Prime Time* last nigh'. An' he said we aren't even spellin' it right. He said there's no 'K'.

— Don't mind him. He can just fuc off.

1-3-12

— See the Monkee's dead.

— Young Damien's monkey?

— Young Damien doesn't have a monkey.

— Does he not? I thought he did.

— No, he doesn't. Not yet an'anyway.

— It's on his list.

— Yeah, but fair play to him. He wants to see if the wallabies survive first. No, your man from the Monkees.

— Davy Jones.

— The English one – yeah.

— The singer.

— Except – there now. What was their one really good song?

— Jaysis. Hey hey we're the—

— No.

— Cheer up sleepy—

— No.

— Then I saw her face.

— Exactly. 'I'm a Believer'. But he didn't sing it.

— Did he not?

— No. Micky Dolenz, the drummer – he sang it.

— So you're saying – wha'? We shouldn't give much of a shite tha' poor oul' Davy's after dyin'?

— No.

— Just because he didn't sing 'I'm a Believer' an' he happens to be English?

— No, I'm not—

— You're fuckin' heartless. My sisters used to love Davy Jones. He did more for Anglo-Irish relations in our gaff than anny of the fuckin' politicians. Him an' Tommy Cooper.

— I only said he didn't sing 'I'm a Believer'.

— An' I didn't sing '24 Hours from Tulsa'. Will you be as fuckin' blasé when I die?

- - - -

— Well?

— Yeh know the way there are no snakes in Ireland?

— Yeah.

— Well, it's not true.

— No?

— Young Damien was tellin' me. People who bought snakes but can't afford them any more. They're releasin' them back into the wild. So—

— Yis went searchin' for snakes.

— A boa constrictor.

— Where?

— Up the mountains. Pine Forest.

— Anny luck?

— Hang on. We brought one o' the wallabies. As bait, like. An' tied him to one o' the trees. It was all very scientific. An' we're sittin' there. An' your man slides right up – an' he coils himself aroun' the wallaby. No complaints from the wallaby.

— Probably thought it was a woman.

— I was thinkin' tha', meself. She has her arms around you, an' by the time yeh know she's stranglin' yeh, you don't really care. So, anyway. The mouth – there's no jaw. It just keeps openin'. Swallows the fuckin' wallaby. An' sits there, digestin' it.

— That's probably why the gangland guys bring the bodies up the mountains.

— Might be. But I was thinkin'. We're sitting there, in this scenery. With the rain an' the sandwiches. An' the boa eatin' the wallaby. Well, there's no other country in the world where yeh'd get tha'.

— You know this Norwegian cunt?

— The guy in court?

— Him – yeah.

— Breivik – or somethin'.

— Yeah.

— What about him?

— Yeh know the way he starts the day with the Nazi salute – his version of it, like?

— Yeah.

— Would you do tha'?

— No.

— Grand.

— Why would I start me day doin' the fuckin' Norwegian Nazi salute?

— So you'll stick with the fartin', yeah?

— Fuck off now.

— It's hard to get your head around it, isn't it?

— Wha'?

— Norwegian Nazis.

— We gave those cunts a hidin' in 1014, an'annyway – in the Battle of Clontarf.

— Tha' was the fuckin' Danes.

— Same thing.

— Is it?

— Not now. Back then, but.

— Really?

— Yeah. Back then, 'Danes' referred to all the Nordies – annyone north of the airport.

— The fuckin' airport?

— Where it is now, yeah.

— So – say – all the fuckers in Dundalk were Danes.

— Yeah. Except worse.

59

— How come?

— Well, yeh know the way the Danes – the genuine ones, like – left Denmark in their fuckin' canoes, so they could pillage an' rape everythin'?

— Yeah.

— Yeah, well, the Dundalk Danes didn't bother leavin'. They just pillaged stuff they already owned and raped their cousins an' their fuckin' cattle an' tha'.

— It hasn't changed, so.

— Not much, no.

16-5-12

— See tha', over there?

— Yeah.

— It's the Opera House, yeah?

— Think so.

— The roof, like. Is it an accident or is it meant to be like tha'?

— How could it be a fuckin' accident?

— Well, it's opera. That's wha' goes on in there. Opera. Singin', like. So you'd have Pavarotti, singin' the World Cup song an' tha' – full blast. And other opera cunts as well. Belting it out. All fuckin' day. So I thought maybe it'd do structural damage. The vibrations, like – eventually.

— No.

— Yeh don't think?

— No. I know what yeh mean, but I'd say they wanted it like tha'. Deliberately fucked up an' stupid-lookin'.

— D'yeh reckon?

— I'd say so.

— An' there's another thing.

— Wha'?

— It's the Sydney Opera House. That's its full name, like.

— Yeah.

— So, like – we're in Sydney.

— Yeah.

— Well. How did we get here?

— Haven't a fuckin' clue.

— Somethin' in the pints, maybe.

— That'd be my fuckin' guess.

The author looks out his hotel window

— See Donna Summer died?

— Did she?

— Yeah.

— That's bad. Wha' was it?

— Cancer.

— Ah well. Cancer of the disco. It gets us all in the end.

— I met the wife durin' 'Love To Love You Baby'.

— You asked her up.

— No.

— No?

— I asked another young one an' she said, Fuck off an' ask me friend.

— An' tha' was the wife.

— Her sister. An' she told me to fuck off as well. So. Annyway. Here we are.

— Grand. She'd a few good songs, but – Donna.

— 'MacArthur Park'. That was me favourite.

— A classic. Until Richard fuckin' Harris took it an' wrecked it.

— It's all it takes, isn't it? Some cunt from Limerick takes a certified disco classic an' turns it into some sort o' bogger lament.

— Someone left the cake out in the rain.

— They wouldn't know wha' cake was in Limerick. They'd be puttin' it in their fuckin' hair.

— An'anyway, they'd've robbed the fuckin' cake long before it started rainin'.

— Is she upset about Donna – the wife?

— Stop. Jesus, man, we were just gettin' over Whitney. An' now this.

— Will she go over for the funeral?

— She's headin' down to the fuckin' credit union.

21-5-12

— See the second-last of the Bee Gees is after dyin'.

— I used to have one o' them suits.

— Wha'?

— One o' the white ones. Like John Travolta's.

— They weren't a bad oul' band.

— Wha' fuckin' eejit ever decided tha' white suits were a good idea?

— Well, you had one.

— Fuck off. I had to – I'd no choice. The weddin'.

— D'yeh still have it?

— Not at all. The state of it – after the weddin', like. It was never goin' to be white again. Or even grey.

— They'd some good songs.

— They'd some big teeth as well.

— D'yeh know wha'? You're a heartless cunt.

— How am I?

— The man dies an' all you can say—

— Fuck up a minute now. Hear me out.

— Go on.

— The songs are great. No question. 'I've Gotta Get a Message To You', 'Night Fever', 'How Can Yeh Mend a Broken Heart'—

— Did they write tha' one?

— There now. I know more about them than you fuckin' do. They'll live a long time – the songs. An' so will the teeth. Long after the rest of him is gone. That's all I'm sayin'.

— So?

— Well, it's depressin', isn't it? The teeth might last longer than the songs.

— Did yeh buy any Facebook shares?

— For fuck sake, m'n. I had to grope behind the fuckin' couch to find the money to pay for this round. Annyway, they're way overpriced.

— I'm not even sure wha' Facebook is.

— A social network.

— What's a fuckin' social network?

— There was a fillum about it.

— *Legally Blonde.*

— That's the one. Anyway, it has millions o' customers – users.

— How's the money made?

— That's the point. Ads. Little ads. But they'll never make their money back. It's like this place. It's a social network as well, really.

— This kip?

— People meet here an' chat – LOL.

— Wha'?

— Never mind.

— There's no little ads here, but.

— That's no problem. We'd just all agree to put in an ad after everythin' we say. Like, Will yeh look at the tits on your one – Fly Emirates.

— Gotcha. Go on.

— So this place might've been worth – wha'? – a million. Before everythin' went mad.

— Okay.

— So then they sell it for ten million. It'll never make sense. We'd never be able to drink the new owners into profit. An' all the bankers an' bondholders who bought Facebook shares at tha' price are a dozy bunch o' cunts – Vorsprung durch Technik.

30-5-12

— Are yeh votin' Yes or No tomorrow?

— No.

— You're votin' No?

— No. I'm not talkin' about it.

— But—

— I'm goin'.

— Hang on – okay. I won't mention it.

— Austerity, me hole. The Yes crowd, righ' – they want us to do wha' the Germans want us to do but the Germans won't fuckin' do wha' they expect us to do. Are yeh with me?

— Yeah—

— So, anyway – historically – doin' what the Germans want yeh to do isn't always a good idea. Fuckin' hell, man, they could make us invade fuckin' Poland the next time we need a dig-out.

— That's a bit far-fetched.

— Exactly wha' the Poles said in 1939. Annyway. There's the No crowd. The anti-austerity brigade.

— Yeah.

— Have yeh ever seen a more miserable-lookin' bunch o' fuckers? They're supposed to be against misery. Half o' them don't even have jackets – an' they never fuckin' smile.

— Mary Lou smiles.

— Only cos she has to.

— Wha'?

— The young Shinners have been trained to smile. So yeh won't think they're goin' to kneecap yeh when you open the door an' they're on the step.

— That's ridiculous.

— I fuckin' agree. But it's true. They've been trained to smile – by the Libyans.

— Wha' d'you make of the football?

— We won't mention Ireland.

— Fair enough.

— Boys in green, me hole.

— We'll move on. I thought Ukraine were a breath o' fresh air.

— Brilliant, yeah.

— Shevchenko, wha'.

— Amazin'. At his age.

— An' he was fuckin' brutal when he was at Chelsea.

— Ah but, when you're playin' for your country.

— Fuckin' McGeady was playin' for his country.

— We won't go there.

— Tha' cunt should be playin' for fuckin' Narnia.

— Shevchenko, but.

— Yeah.

— He— Don't get me wrong now. An' listen. This is between ourselves.

— Go on.

— Well, like. I've never fancied a man in me life.

— Go on.

— But. If I ever did fancy a man – if I could. It'd be Shevchenko.

— I'm the same with Torres.

— You fancy Torres?

— I do, yeah.

— But he's shite. You're always sayin' it.

— He is. It's fuckin' tragic. But it's more of a paternal thing, I think. I just want to cuddle him. Tell him it'll be grand, he's not half as shite as he looks. Is it the same with you an' Shevchenko?

— Not really – no.

— Grand.

— Wha' about the Irish lads? Could yeh see yourself cuddlin' anny o' them?

— It's your round.

— You must've given Torres a fair oul' cuddle before our match against Spain, did yeh?

— Fuck off, you.

— You must've well an' truly—

— One more fuckin' word an' I'll be lettin' your missis know you're thinkin' of Andriy Shevchenko every night when you're slidin' into the fuckin' bed.

— Keep your voice down, for fuck—

— Fuck off.

— It's not true.

— Just fuck off.

— It's not.

— Grand.

— Wha' d'yeh think of Theo Walcott?

— As a footballer?

— Ah, for fuck sake! Yes! As a fuckin' footballer!

— Yeh know what's happened?

— Keep your fuckin' voice down.

— You've ruined it.

— Wha' – how?

— With your Shevchenko revelations. We'll never be able to talk about the football again. There's the quarter-finals, the semis, the final, the new season comin' up – the rest of our fuckin' lives. It's *Brokeback* fuckin' *Mountain*.

— Not at all – calm down. Listen. Wha' d'yeh think of Ronaldo?

— Selfish little step-over cunt. There's no disputin' his talent but he doesn't give a shite about his team. He plays for Ronaldo an' he disappears on the big occasions.

— Brilliant. Great analysis. Wasn't so hard, was it?

— No.

— So. Movin' on. Wha' d'yeh make of Oxlade-Chamberlain?

— He's—

— Yeah – go on.

— He's lovely.

— See the Queen is back.

— Wha' queen?

— The Queen of fuckin' England. What other queen is there?

— Where is she?

— Here.

— Where?

— The North.

— That's not here.

— Yes, it is.

— No, it isn't. It's England.

— Northern Ireland is England?

— Yeah.

— That's fuckin' mad.

— It belongs to England.

— No, it—

— Do you want it?

— No.

— Shut up then. What's she doin' up there, an'anyway?

— Shakin' hands with McGuinness.

— God love her. At least his hands'll be nice an' soft.

— Wha'?

— The gun oil.

— Ah, for fuck sake—

— They all use it up there. It's great for the hands. All the massage parlours – they use it.

— I'm not listenin'.

— They butter their fuckin' bread with it.

— Not listenin'.

— Will he tell her a joke?

— Wha'?

— McGuinness.

— I doubt it.

— Get her to laugh, like he did with Paisley. Here, Your Majesty, did yeh hear the one abou' the priest an' the donkey?

— He says he won't be callin' her Your Majesty.

— That's a pity. Cos it's a great joke. An' she loves donkeys.

— Horses.

— Same thing.

— See the weather in England?

— Fuck the weather in England. We've loads of our own.

— It's unbelievable.

— Desperate.

— Fuckin' relentless.

— But I'll tell yeh. It's handy enough for the polar bear.

— The polar bear?

— Young Damien's.

— You gave in.

— Ah, yeah.

— You're a gobshite.

— Ah now. He's grand. He's only a pup.

— Young Damien?

— The bear.

— It's a cub.

— Wha'?

— Not a pup. Seals have pups.

— Don't remind me.

— Is the bear in the house with yis?

— God, no. He's ou' the back. An' happy enough, in all the rain an' tha'.

— Wha' d'yis feed him?

— You can smell it, can yeh?

— Wha'?

— I rubbed half a lemon all over meself. Stung like fuck as well.

— Why did yeh do tha'?

— To get rid o' the smell.

— Wha' smell?

— Whale.

— Jesus, m'n. Did yeh buy him a fuckin' whale as well?

— No way – no. We heard it on the news. A dead whale on the beach.

— Where?

— Sligo.

— Yeh went to fuckin' Sligo?

— That's where the fuckin' whale was. They don't sell them in SuperValu.

— Yeh spent the day cuttin' up a whale?

— Most of it was gone by the time we got there. But we got a good vanful.

— See your man from Deep Purple died.

   — Cancer again. Did yeh like them?

   — No. Well, yeah. They were brilliant.

   — 'Smoke on the Water'.

   — Tha' one takes me back.

   — Go on.

   — I was seventeen.

   — Like Janis Ian.

   — Fuck off. I was in this place called Club 74.

   — I remember it.

   — 'Smoke on the Water' was playin' an' I was with this young one, an' she had a few rum an' blacks in her. Annyway, her tongue was all over me face. But she eventually finds me mouth. So – grand. The national anthem comes on and I say, We'll give it a miss, will we? An' we're out o' there an' straight into St Anne's.

   — Now we're talkin'.

   — Listen. She leans back against a tree. Her own idea, now. One thing leads to another – I couldn't fuckin' believe it. An' I'll tell yeh, when I—

   — Came.

   — Exactly. I thought I'd never stop. Premier Dairies couldn't've kept up with the demand.

   — An' what about her?

   — She'd gone.

   — Wha'?

   — She wasn't there.

   — So, hang on – wha'? You're tellin' me yeh rode the arse off a tree?

   — Basically.

   — Jaysis. Wha' sort of tree was it?

   — Don't know. I don't know much abou' trees.

— It's was Magnums all round in our place tonigh'.

— How come?

— My young one's fella – young Damien's dad, like. I told yeh about him.

— Yeah.

— He got ou' today.

— Great.

— An' he already has a job.

— Go 'way. Doin' wha'?

— Security.

— Great. Where?

— The Olympics. In London, like.

— Fuckin' hell. How did tha' happen?

— Well, the security company tha' got the contract—

— G4S.

— They've been makin' a balls of it. Their own staff aren't turnin' up an' the army lads over there don't want the gig either cos they signed up to shoot Iraqis an' tha'.

— Grand. So what'll he be guardin'?

— Sand.

— Fuckin' sand?

— The beach volleyball sand. It's special. They don't use the stuff off the beach. The Yanks would object to broken glass an' condoms an' tha'. The stadium isn't ready but the sand is.

— So he'll be guardin' sand.

— No.

— Hang on, you – no?

— He sold it.

— Wha'?

— He's buddies with a chap who knows a fella who's got the job fixin' some o' them houses with the pyrite,

75

yeh know. So they're headin' over to London with a lurry.

— What'll the poor beach volleyball young ones do?
— They'll have to go to the fuckin' beach.

30-7-12

— Were yeh watchin' the women's archery?

— Missed it.

— Big girls with bows an' arrows.

— Grand.

— The bows – fuckin' hell. They're like out of a video game. The type o' thing yeh'd bring with yeh into a room full o' Batman fans.

— Fuckin' stop tha'.

— Wha'?

— Stop.

— How's the polar bear?

— It's interestin'.

— Yeah?

— Well, the weather's picked up, so he's strugglin' a bit. She gives him the ice out of her fuckin' mojitos an' I was thinkin' o' bringin' him in to watch the synchronised divin'. Thought it might remind him o' home. The water an' tha'.

— Makes sense.

— No.

— No?

— Not accordin' to young Damien. He doesn't know he's a polar bear, Granda, he says. An' he explains it me – his experiment, like.

— Go on.

— We're – the humans, like – we're the only ones tha' know wha' we are. The animals haven't a clue. So why should a polar bear struggle in the heat if he doesn't even know he's supposed to be cold?

— Hang on—

— So we're pretendin' he's a dog. See how it goes. Took him ou' for a walk an' all.

— An'?
— He killed a couple o' dogs.
— That's encouragin'.
— Young Damien was pleased enough.

31-7-12

— See Maeve Binchy died.

   — Sad tha'.

   — It is, isn't it? D'yeh ever read any of her bukes?

   — No.

   — Me neither.

   — I read the covers. In the bed, like. Whenever she had her hands on a new Maeve Binchy buke, yeh knew it was goin' to be a quiet fuckin' night.

   — Same in our place.

   — Still, but. No hard feelin's.

   — No.

   — I liked her on the radio.

   — Yeah. I was thinkin' tha' meself earlier, when the news was on, like. I was lookin' ou' the kitchen window. An' young Damien was ou' there, sittin' in the deckchair, yeh know – takin' notes. Watchin' the polar bear peelin' the skin off o' Larry Hennessey's new English bulldog. An' I said to meself, Maeve would've seen the funny side o' tha'.

   — I know wha' yeh mean.

   — Wha' for us would be just a normal everyday domestic scene. She would've made it look funny.

   — Exactly.

8-8-12

— You're in early.

— So are you.

— I need a fuckin' pint.

— You were watchin' Katie Taylor, yeah?

— Brilliant.

— Fuckin' brilliant.

— Did yeh ever think watchin' a girl boxin' the head off another girl would make yeh feel so proud?

— Gas, isn't it?

— Will she win the gold but?

— Foregone conclusion.

— No doubts at all?

— None.

— How come?

— She's from Bray.

— Wha'?

— Did yeh ever walk through Bray on a Saturday nigh', did yeh?

— No.

— It's either boxin' or sprintin'.

— Makes sense. See the Brits were claimin' her, but. The *Daily Telegraph* or somethin'.

— Never mind the Brits. We'll start worryin' if the Germans start claimin' her.

— Or the IMF – we'll eliminate the debt in exchange for Katie Taylor.

— No deal, lads. We'll take the debt.

— She's ours.

— She is.

— An' see your man, the showjumper – the one with the horse tha' cheated – he's doin' well too.

— Fuck'm.

— Yeah.

9-8-12

— Jesus, man – me heart.

    — It was close.

    — Jesus –

    — But she won.

    — She's brilliant.

    — Just brilliant.

    — I love her.

    — Me too. Your man on the telly's right. She's a fuckin' legend.

    — She's a born-again Christian as well. Did yeh know tha'?

    — God is my shield – yeah. That's what's made her a gold medallist.

    — Wha'?

    — The religion.

    — Wha'?

    — No, listen. If she was a Catholic, righ', she'd've been happy with the bronze.

    — Wha'?!

    — It's always the same. We qualify for somethin' or we get to a final or a semi-final and that's grand – we're there for the fuckin' party. But the born-agains – Jesus.

    — You're serious.

    — It was the same with the War of Independence. We won three-quarters o' the country and then we said, That'll do us. An' we went home for our fuckin' tea.

    — But if we'd been born-again Christians, we'd've kept goin'?

    — The fourth green field, yeah – no bother. And on into Scotland – an' Iceland – an' fuckin' Zimbabwe.

    — Yeh might be righ'.

    — Think about it.

    — When was the last time we won a gold without cheatin'?

— Twenty years – Michael Carruth.
— So maybe honesty is the best policy.
— Ah now – calm down.

— Pussy Riot.

    — That's just middle age. It'll sort itself ou'.

    — No. The Russian young ones. The group, like.

    — What abou' them?

    — I can't get me head around it. Hooliganism motivated by religious hatred. What the fuck is tha'?

    — It's just the excuse.

    — Wha'?

    — It's nothin' to do with religion. They're in jail cos Putin doesn't like them.

    — Is that all?

    — Listen. Remember punk – back in the day, like?

    — The Sex Pistols. 'God Save the Queen' an' tha'.

    — Exactly.

    — Brilliant.

    — I wasn't mad about it meself. But annyway. It blew the other music away.

    — Glam rock.

    — Putin loves it.

    — Wha'?

    — Glam rock.

    — Fuck off.

    — Serious. He's mad into Gary Glitter.

    — Tha' makes sense. They prob'ly like the same videos.

    — Ah now. Annyway. Fuckin' Putin an' the other cunts in the Politburo all have platforms an' silver suits, an' he mimes along to 'I'm the Leader of the Gang' an' 'Do Yeh Wanna Touch Me?'.

    — Ah, fuck off.

    — I'm tellin' yeh. He's been doin' it for years. He fuckin' hates punk.

— An' that's why those young ones are in jail?

— The Pistols made Gary Glitter look ridiculous an' those three young ones make Putin look even more ridiculous.

— See the *Top Gun* fella died.

— Tom Cruise?

— No, the director. Tony Scott. Killed himself.

— I seen that alrigh'. It's sad.

— It is, yeah. D'yeh ever see *Top Gun*?

— God, no. No fuckin' way. I put the foot down after *Flashdance*.

— Good man.

— Had to be done. Hand on me heart now – I've never seen a fillum with Tom Cruise in it.

— None o' them?

— Not fuckin' one.

— Not even the *Mission: Impossibles*?

— Is he in them?

— Yeah – 'course.

— Well, I've seen them alrigh'. But I never noticed him.

— He's there alrigh'.

— For fuck sake. He was chargin' around so much an' bashin' into glass, I never saw his fuckin' face. Are yeh sure about this?

— Yeah, yeah. He's in all o' them. He's the star, like.

— Fuck – I feel a bit violated now.

— Still but. Those action fillums – it doesn't really matter who's in them, sure it doesn't?

— Unless it's one o' the *Die Hards*.

— Ah, but they're different.

— Cos o' Bruce.

— He's one o' the lads.

— Yippee-ki-yay, motherfucker.

— He was in here takin' notes before he went to Hollywood.

— He fuckin' was.

— How's young Damien gettin' on?

— Well –

— Yeah?

— He was a bit low in himself.

— After yis buried the polar bear?

— Maybe a life o' science isn't for me, Granda, he says. Broke me fuckin' heart.

— I can imagine.

— So – yeah. But then. He starts cuttin' up stuff – bits o' cloth, like. An' he asks for the lend of his granny's sewin' machine.

— Oh Jesus.

— Yeah –

— You're worried.

— I *was*. I'm ashamed to admit it. I think the world of him – he's a great little lad. But annyway, he's lookin' at magazines and chattin' to the granny an' tellin' her all his fashion ideas.

— God—

— Now, I'd never want to interfere with his – like, his natural leanin's. You with me?

— Yeah.

— But I did.

— How?

— I bought him a tiger. A cub, like.

— To turn him away from the sewin' machine?

— I hated meself. When I realised what I was up to. But I needn't've worried.

— How come?

— He went to school this mornin' wearin' a little tiger-skin waistcoat.

— He made it himself?

— He smelt like the back o' the chipper after a long weekend. But I'll tell yeh—

— Naomi Campbell will be wearin' his stuff.

— She'll be fuckin' lucky.

— Did yeh see your man winnin' his medal last nigh'?

— Brilliant.

— What's his name again?

— McKillop.

— Wasn't he brilliant?

— Fuckin' amazin'.

— But I'll tell yeh – the bit tha' got me. When his ma – like, when his ma presented him with the medal. I was nearly cryin'.

— It was a fuckin' disgrace.

— Wha'?!

— Did yeh not hear?

— Hear wha'?

— The story.

— Wha' fuckin' story? If you're—

— Just listen, will yeh.

— Go on.

— Righ'. They had Kylie Minogue lined up to give the poor lad his medal.

— Fuck off.

— Serious.

— Jesus. Why Kylie, but?

— Ah, for fuck –. Listen. Say you've just won a medal. There's an Oul' Lads Olympics an' you've won gold for – say – the synchronised arse scratchin'. Okay?

— Okay.

— Can yeh think of annyone you'd prefer to see comin' at yeh with your medal than Kylie?

— No.

— Well, that's wha' they had set up for poor McKillop.

— You're fuckin' messin'.

— It's on YouTube. His ma pushed Kylie out o' the

way – split her head open against one o' the pillars. And she walked ou' with the fuckin' medal.

— Fuck off.

— Poor Kylie needed stitches.

— I'm not listenin'.

— Made me ashamed to be Irish.

— Fuck off.

Roddy Doyle was born in Dublin in 1958. He is the author of nine acclaimed novels, two collections of short stories, and *Rory & Ita*, a memoir about his parents. He won the Booker Prize in 1993 for *Paddy Clarke Ha Ha Ha*.